Duck and Hippo
LOST AND FOUND

By **JONATHAN LONDON**   Illustrated by **ANDREW JOYNER**

two lions

Published by Two Lions, New York

www.apub.com

Amazon, the Amazon logo, and Two Lions are trademarks of Amazon.com, Inc., or its affiliates.

ISBN-13: 9781542045629
ISBN-10: 1542045629

The illustrations are rendered in brush and ink with wash and pencil and then digitally colored.
Book design by Abby Dening

Printed in China
First Edition
1 3 5 7 9 10 8 6 4 2

For Sean & Steph, Aaron, and sweet Maureen
—J. L.

For Lloyd and Carolyn
—A. J.

To celebrate the end of summer,
Duck and Hippo invited their friends
Turtle, Elephant, and Pig to a picnic
at their favorite pond.

"*Yippee!*" sang Duck
on her way to the pond with Hippo.
She skipped and danced around him,
swinging a basket full of goodies.

When they arrived, their friends were waiting.
And each had something to share.

Elephant had brought peppermint peach juice and a giant watermelon.

Pig had brought an extra-large pickle-and-pineapple pizza.

And Turtle had brought a picnic basket filled with paper plates and cups, a blanket, and honey barbecue chips.

Duck said, "Let the celebrations BEGIN!"

Then Elephant blew
water out of his trunk.

SPLOOOOOOOSH!

Duck popped open her umbrella
and danced and sang beneath it.

"IT'S RAINING! IT'S POURING!
THE OLD TURTLE IS SNORRRING!"

Turtle pulled his head into his shell.
And Pig TWIRLED in
her blue swimsuit
on Turtle's back.

But Hippo said,
"WAIT!"

Everybody stopped what they were doing.

"Excuse me," Hippo said,
"but I can't celebrate!
I forgot to bring something
to share for the picnic!"

"It's okay, Hippo," said Duck.
"We have plenty of food."

"It is NOT okay!" said Hippo.
"I didn't bring ANYTHING!
And I'm so hungry
I could eat an elephant!

"Oops! Sorry, dear Elephant."

"NO PROBLEM!"
boomed Elephant.

"I know!" said Hippo,
getting an idea.
"I'll go and pick some wild berries—
the last berries of summer!"

"That's so *sweet!*"
said Duck.

"Hurry!" said Pig. "I'm *starving!*"
"Take your time," said Turtle.
"Take your time."

Hippo bowed politely,
then marched off into the forest.

But he was gone for a very long time
and Duck began to worry.

"Maybe he's *lost!*" said Duck.
"Let's go look for him."

So they all went into the forest to look for Hippo.

"Hippo! OH, HIPPO! Where *are* you?" yelled Duck.

And everybody joined in. "Hippo! OH, HIPPO! Where *are* you?"

But Hippo did not call back.
He was still looking for berries.

He searched both ends of the rainbow
under a waterfall.

But there were no berries.

Duck and her friends
looked and looked for Hippo.
The sun was going down
and the moon was coming up.

Duck worried: *It's getting dark!*
What if Hippo fell in a hole
and can't climb out?

"Hippo!
OH, HIPPO!
Where *are* you?"
yelled Duck.

And everybody joined in.
"Hippo! OH, HIPPO! Where *are* you?"

But Hippo did not call back.
He was still searching for berries.
He climbed a small mountain in the moonlight . . .

ZOOOOM!

and slid down the other side.

But there were *still* no berries.

Just then the moon hid behind a cloud.
It got darker than ever.

Now Duck and her friends
were in almost total darkness.

"Hippo! OH, HIPPO!
Where *are* you?" yelled Duck.

And everybody joined in.
"Hippo! OH, HIPPO! Where *are* you?"

And *this* time Hippo called back.
It sounded like

"HEELLLLP!"

But it was so dark that
Duck and her friends couldn't see anything!
Until …

the moon burst out from behind the clouds . . .

and there was Hippo, yelling,

"HELLOOOO!"

"Hippo! OH, HIPPO!" cried Duck.
"Were you *lost*?"

"NOOO!" said Hippo....

"*I was* FOUND!

"Thank you, dear Duck,
for coming to find me!"

"And look what *I* just found," said Hippo.
"One for each of you, my friends . . .
the last berries of summer!"

"Now we can *eat!*" said Pig.
"Let's hurry back to the picnic.
I'm *starving!*"

"Take your time," said Turtle.
"Take your time."

"NO PROBLEM!"

boomed Elephant.
"I'll help speed things up!"

And he lifted Turtle with his trunk
and carried him on his shoulder.

When they got back to the picnic, Duck said,

"Let the celebrations BEGIN!"

Then she offered Hippo a plate
and joked, "*Quackers* and cheese?"

"Thank you, dear Duck! But what I *really* want . . .

is PIZZA!"

"*Yippee!*" sang Duck.

It was the end of summer.
And *how* they did celebrate!

"HIP—HIPPO—RAAY!"